THE COOKIE LOVED 'ROUND THE WORLD

The Story of the Chocolate Chip Cookie

By

KATHLEEN TEAHAN

Tammy and Claire,

Follow your dreams!

Kathy Teahan

The Cookie Loved 'Round the World: The Story of the Chocolate Chip Cookie, Published August, 2017

Interior and Cover Illustrations: Larisa Hart
Interior Design & Cover Layout: Howard Johnson
Editorial and Proofreading: Eden Rivers Editorial Services; Karen Grennan
Photo Credits:
Nestlé, image of Nestlé Semi-Sweet Morsels, page 25
Tracy Seelye, image of Whitman Center giant cookie, page 36
Stanley Bauman, image of Ken and Ruth Wakefield, page 37
Jake O'Callaghan, author photo, page 38
Nestlé and Toll House are registered trademarks of Société des Produits Nestlé S.A., Vevey, Switzerland.

Published by SDP Publishing, an imprint of SDP Publishing Solutions, LLC.

For more information about this book contact Lisa Akoury-Ross at SDP Publishing by email at info@SDPPublishing.com.

SDP Publishing
Permissions Department
PO Box 26, East Bridgewater, MA 02333
or email your request to info@SDPPublishing.com.

ISBN-13 (print): 978-0-9968426-3-1
ISBN-13 (ebook): 978-0-9968426-4-8

Printed in the United States of America

To my grandchildren—Jill,
Casey, Hadley, Grayson, and
Emmet—and all children
that they may have enough
nutritious food to grow into
happy, healthy adults; enough
cookies to enjoy; and enough love
to fill all their days.

Acknowledgments

Thank you to my parents, Florence and Joseph Keras; my eight siblings; my late husband, Bob Teahan; my children Anne, Jean, Bob, and John; and my five grandchildren. Their love inspires me every day.

Thank you to: the late Ruth Wakefield who created the chocolate chip cookie in her beautiful Toll House Restaurant; Nancy L'Heureux's 1997 third grade students from the Chace Elementary School, Somerset, Massachusetts, for reminding me how remarkable the chocolate chip cookie is; my son, Bob, whose early sketches inspired me to pursue this project; my cousin, Bob Tonello, for providing photographs of my late Aunt Ann, the narrator of our story; my friends, especially Christine Conway-Maiorano and Jane Travers-Morgan, whose excitement about the cookie book and memories about the Toll House Restaurant kept me writing; to the Whitman Historical Society for preserving materials about the Toll House Restaurant and cookie story; John Campbell, who searched through files and boxes to find Toll House artifacts and information; Senator Tom Norton, who asked me to sponsor the state cookie bill; Whitman educators and students who told women's history and supported our efforts to memorialize Ruth Wakefield and her famous cookie; Sr. Kathleen Short, CSJ, who pointed out the correlation of hunger to violence and crime; Tracy Seelye, photographer and editor of the Whitman and Hanson Express, for her photograph of Whitman's "Giant Cookie Drop"; Deborah Poole-Anderson, publisher of the *Whitman-Hanson Express* and *Plympton-Halifax Express* for research on the "Giant Cookie" and for recommending Lari, my wonderful illustrator; Jake O'Callaghan, for taking my picture for the author page; the Independent Association of Framingham State Alumni, for assistance researching Ruth Graves Wakefield, a 1924 Graduate of Framingham Normal School (currently Framingham State University); Stonehill College Archives and Historical Collections, for preserving and sharing Stanley Bauman's Toll House photographs; the Cape Cod Writers Center, for their encouragement and enthusiasm; Société des Produits Nestlé S.A., Vevey, Switzerland, for the right to use the trade names Nestlé and Toll House Chocolate Chip Cookie; Roz O'Hearn, Director, Communications and Brand Affairs at Nestlé, who since 1997, has provided much assistance with my Toll House cookie projects.

And last I would like to thank the entire production and publishing team: my illustrator, Larisa Hart, whose artwork truly brought this story to life; to my publisher Lisa Akoury-Ross, who guided me through the complications of book publishing; my editor, Lisa Schleipfer, whose professionalism and creativity blended with my ideas to create a very "delicious" story; my designer, Howard Johnson, for combining all of our "ingredients" for this book perfectly.

This book was truly a team effort. Thank you, Team Toll House!

Hello. My name is Ann, but my twenty-five nieces and nephews call me Aunt Ann. You can too.

I love chocolate chip cookies, don't you? I'm here to tell you a very delicious story. One about the very first chocolate chip cookie ever made.

The Great Depression

The year was 1933 and I was eight years old. On Sunday mornings my brother Bob and I sold about one hundred Sunday papers in front of Holy Ghost Church in Whitman, Massachusetts. Every Saturday, our mother made sixty dozen donuts in her three extra-large, black cast iron skillets.

Bob and I pulled his red wagon through our Stetson Street neighborhood and sold my mother's delicious homemade donuts for five cents a dozen. We each got to keep a nickel and the rest of the money helped pay the family bills.

It was tough times for us during the Great Depression. My father's job was one of 4,000 eliminated at the Quincy Fore River Shipyard. All family members, of all ages, had to help earn money to pay the bills.

Historical Ingredients

The Great Depression was a hungry and hard time for many Americans. Today many people still struggle with hunger.

An estimated 15 million children in the US lived in food insecure households in 2014.[1]

In 2015 throughout the world, there were 795 million people who did not have enough food to lead a healthy, active life.[2]

[1] Whitmore Schanzenbach, Diane, Lauren Bauer, and Greg Nantz. 2016. "Twelve facts about food insecurity and SNAP." The Brookings Institution. Accessed May 2016. https://www.brookings.edu/research/twelve-facts-about-food-insecurity-and-snap/

[2] World Food Programme. 2015. "World Hunger Falls To Under 800 Million, Eradication Is Next Goal." World Food Programme. Accessed May 2016. https://www.wfp.org/news/news-release/world-hunger-falls-under-800-million-eradication-next-goal-0

Times were extremely tough during that Great Depression, but we had *resilience*, a big word my father used that meant an attitude of not giving up. It also meant appreciating what you had and believing that better days were coming as a result of your hard work and *determination*, meaning you continued to do what you set out to do even when problems occurred.

I have a true story about how hard work and determination made good things happen. This story begins during the Depression in my hometown of Whitman.

The Toll House Restaurant

It all started one morning with a shortage of walnuts in the Toll House Restaurant kitchen.

"Mrs. Wakefield, what are we going to do? Last month there was a sugar shortage. Today, we have no walnuts for the Butter Do Drop cookies that I'm scheduled to bake for the Corcoran wedding reception here tomorrow. We can't disappoint the bride and groom and all their guests!" complained Bernice, the Toll House Restaurant baker.

In 1930, Ruth Wakefield, a dietician who graduated from Framingham Normal School, and her husband, Ken, spent their life savings to buy a Cape Cod style house. In this house, the Wakefields opened a small restaurant with only seven tables, and they called it the Toll House Restaurant.

It is believed that many years before, there was a small building across the street where tolls were collected from travelers on their way from New Bedford to Boston. The Wakefields thought naming their restaurant the "Toll House" would be good for business.

The large dining room had a tree growing right through it, with branches that were sticking through the roof! It was a beautiful elm tree that originally was part of a patio. The Wakefields built an entire room—the Garden Room—around the tree.

 **Historical Ingredients**

A Unique Dining Experience

Wanting to make customers remember their times at the Toll House as outstanding, all the silver coins used to give change went through the dishwasher until they were as shiny as could be!

During the first years the Toll House was open for business—from 1930 through 1939—America was experiencing the Great Depression. There was a great shortage of work for adults and an even greater shortage of food. Some families ate dandelion sandwiches and dandelion soup. Some grew vegetables in the median strip of grass between the sidewalk and the street in front of their homes.

Historical Ingredients

The Great Depression was caused by growing inequality of incomes, the Dust Bowl that ruined farming in the West, and the 1929 Stock Market Crash. By 1932, twenty-five percent of workers were unemployed, and there was a shortage of both food and money to buy food.

Now, there are many versions of how Ruth Wakefield created
the chocolate chip cookies, and this one is my favorite!

Mrs. Wakefield thought about the cookie problem. "Hmm, we need an ingredient to substitute for the walnuts, something with a distinctive flavor." She named possible ingredients: "raisins, dates, peanuts ..." Suddenly, a block of Nestlé™ semisweet chocolate on the counter caught her eye. She broke chunks of it into the cookie dough. "Let's see what some chocolate will do in our Do Drops recipe!"

A mouth-watering aroma filled the restaurant kitchen as the experimental batch of cookies baked. Bernice removed the cookies from the oven and exclaimed, "Well, look at that! The chocolate didn't melt and spread in the batter. It is still in chunks in the cookies."

 ## Historical Ingredients

There are many stories of how the chocolate chip cookie was invented. Some of them are:

- Ruth wrote the recipe for chocolate chip cookies while riding on an airplane.

- The bakers were trying to make chocolate cookies, and the chunks of chocolate just didn't melt in the batter.

- The kitchen ran out of butter, so they tried chocolate instead.

"Are we ready for the taste test?" Ruth Wakefield asked as she passed a plate of warm cookies around to the chef, sous-chef, salad and dessert girls, waitresses, busboys, and dishwashers. There was a smile on every face as the Toll House staff gave two thumbs up to the new cookie.

The popularity with customers was immediate. Soon it became the restaurant's signature cookie, The Toll House Chocolate Crunch Cookie. One day, as Mrs. Wakefield watched the bakers using an ice pick to break chunks off the block of chocolate, she had another idea. If the chocolate could be produced in small pieces, her bakers could work faster and cookie production would speed up.

ORIGINAL RECIPE
..se CHOCOLATE COOKIES

...ter, add
...own sugar
...anulated
    sugar and
...eaten whole.
...oda in
...t water, and mix
...sp. salt. Lastly
...hopped nuts
    and...

2 Economy sized
bars Nestlé's semi-
sweet chocolate
which have been
cut into pieces the
size of a pea.
Flavor with 1 tsp.
vanilla and drop
by half teaspoons
on a greased cookie
sheet. Bake 10-12
minutes in 375° oven.

Mrs. Wakefield contacted the Nestlé Chocolate Company about her idea. It wasn't long before their food engineers devised a way to produce small bits of chocolate. In 1939, Nestlé took its semisweet chocolate bar and scored it—meaning they cut the bars, but not all the way through—into 160 pieces that easily would separate into smaller pieces to use in the cookies.

Shortly after that, Nestlé created individual small teardrop-shaped pieces of chocolate and called them *morsels*. Their artists created a bright-yellow cellophane bag to hold the morsels and printed the Toll House™ cookie recipe on the bag.

 Historical Ingredients

Did you know?

Nestlé not only still prints the recipe on bags of their chocolate chips, but they also still refer to the chips as "morsels."

In 1939, Nestlé sold their first Nestlé Toll House chocolate morsels. Families all over America were baking chocolate chip cookies. During World War II, women sent their sons and boyfriends and husbands packages containing homemade chocolate chip cookies.

 Historical Ingredients

Care packages are still a popular way to help support our American servicemen and servicewomen. There are organizations that collect snacks, letters, cards, toiletries like soap and toothbrushes—and of course, chocolate chip cookies—to send to our troops in the United States and overseas!

While serving our country all over the world, soldiers, sailors, air force cadets, and marines felt the love and support of home as they tasted and shared those chocolate chip cookies.

Students with an Idea

For years, this small town cookie's popularity grew and grew. Then, in 1997, a third grade class from Somerset, Massachusetts attempted to have the chocolate chip cookie named the official Massachusetts cookie. As part of a school project, these third graders had polled students in their school to determine their favorite cookie. They even made graphs to show the results. The chocolate chip cookie won by a landslide.

 Historical Ingredients

Before becoming president, Senator John F. Kennedy often stopped for supper at the Toll House on his trips between Boston and his family's summer home on Cape Cod. He looked forward to a yummy chocolate chip cookie after his meal and purchased some to bring to the Kennedy clan in Hyannis. That was a lot of cookies!

Next, they took out a loan to purchase ingredients, determined what to charge for the cookies in order to make a profit, and created advertisements for their sales. They decided to donate profits from the cookie sale to a local food pantry.

When State Senator Thomas Norton visited the class, he challenged the third graders to petition the Massachusetts Legislature to make the chocolate chip cookie the official state cookie of Massachusetts.

The Joint Committee on State Administration held a hearing at the Massachusetts State House in Boston to determine if the chocolate chip cookie was an important symbol of Massachusetts history and culture.

These hearings are part of the process a formal committee of senators and representatives use to determine whether to recommend a *bill* to the Senate or House for a vote by all the members. Interestingly, anyone in Massachusetts can file a bill to be considered.

 *Historical Ingredients*

States designate certain flowers, birds, animals, and foods as their official *state symbols*. These symbols are meaningful to the state's people because they represent the culture and unique character of each state.

At hearings like this one, people for and against an idea speak to support their opinions. During the hearing, Peter Koutoujian, the representative for Newton, Massachusetts, argued in favor of making the fig cookie the state cookie. The people of Newton were proud of the cookie named for their town.

However, a third grader gave the winning argument for the chocolate chip cookie when she said, "Whoever came home from school and was all excited to smell a fig cookie baking in the kitchen?"

Several students, a few representatives, senators, and other interested people spoke for or against the bill. Eventually, the cookie bill went to the Senate and then the House where it passed unanimously.

The Official Cookie of Massachusetts

July 9, 1997, was a very big day for this small-town cookie! On that day, Governor William Weld signed the law—which was co-sponsored by Senators Tom Norton and Joan Menard, and State Representative Kathy Teahan—making the chocolate chip cookie the official cookie of the Commonwealth of Massachusetts.

2   SENATE — No. 1716   [March 1997]

By Mr. Norton, a petition (accompanied by bill, Senate, No. 1716) of Thomas C. Norton, Kathleen M. Teahan and others for legislation to designate the chocolate chip cookie as the official cookie of the Commonwealth. State Administration.

The Commonwealth of Massachusetts

In the Year One Thousand Nine Hundred and Ninety-Seven.

AN ACT DESIGNATING THE CHOCOLATE CHIP COOKIE AS THE OFFICIAL COOKIE OF THE COMMONWEALTH.

Be it enacted by the Senate and House of Representatives in General Court assembled, and by the authority of the same, as follows:

1   SECTION 1. Chapter 2 of the General Laws is hereby amended
2 by adding after section 39 the following new section:—
3   Section 40. The chocolate chip cookie shall be the official
4 cookie of the Commonwealth.

The people of Whitman were so proud and excited that they held a Toll House Cookie Day with a small parade. The middle school band played, and children dressed like bakers, cookies, and cartons of milk. There was a reunion of Toll House Restaurant workers, speeches by politicians, and the presentation of a check to Jim Davidson, Chairman of the Whitman Food Pantry.

Of course, there was a Toll House Cookie bake sale. Nestlé donated all the cookie dough for it. Nestlé also donated $50,000.00 for a new playground and improvements to the Whitman Town Park.

Sixteen years later, on December 31, 2013, a giant, illuminated metal chocolate chip cookie, designed and built by students of South Shore Vocational Technical High School, dropped from a tall, fire truck ladder in Whitman Center to mark the beginning of the New Year. This First Night celebration in Whitman also marked the 75th Anniversary of the creation of Nestlé semisweet chocolate morsels.

Just like I never tire of eating chocolate chip cookies, I never get tired of telling this story about a "small town" cookie that became loved around the world. Working at the Toll House Restaurant was a cookie lover's dream. When Ken and Ruth Wakefield invested their life savings to live out their dream and open a restaurant, little did they know that vision would lead Ruth to create the famous and popular chocolate chip cookie. Her goals and her positive attitude transformed a common butter cookie in the small town of Whitman into a famous cookie loved 'round the world. I hope you will live out your dreams and tell lots of your own stories.

About The Author

Kathleen Teahan is a retired teacher and Massachusetts legislator. While working her way through college, one of her summer jobs was as a salad girl at the Toll House Restaurant in Whitman, Massachusetts. She taught English at Whitman-Hanson Regional High School and the Gordon Mitchell Middle School in East Bridgewater, Massachusetts, where her eighth grade students wrote picture books for third grade partners. Reading always has been her pleasure and she enjoys watching her grandchildren develop a love of reading. She enjoys creating stories for her grandchildren.

Social justice is a passion for Teahan. She served on the Whitman School Committee for six years. In the past, she volunteered in classrooms, food programs, scholarship committees, and several outreach programs including Habitat for Humanity. Throughout her years in the legislature, she worked for justice, quality education for all, improved health—especially oral health—and equal rights. Her goal is to leave a better world for her grandchildren and children throughout the world.

Kathleen Teahan was married to the late Bob Teahan from 1971 to 1997. She is the mother of Anne Teahan-Dunning, Jean, Bob, and John Teahan, and is blessed with two daughters-in-law and five grandchildren. She is presently finishing a memoir about her ten years in the Massachusetts legislature.

THE COOKIE LOVED 'ROUND THE WORLD
The Story of the Chocolate Chip Cookie
Kathleen Teahan

Publisher: SDP Publishing

Also available in ebook format

Available at all major bookstores

SDP Publishing

www.SDPPublishing.com
Contact us at: info@SDPPublishing.com

CPSIA information can be obtained at www.ICGtesting.com
Printed in the USA
BVIW12n2314210917
495058BV00001B/1